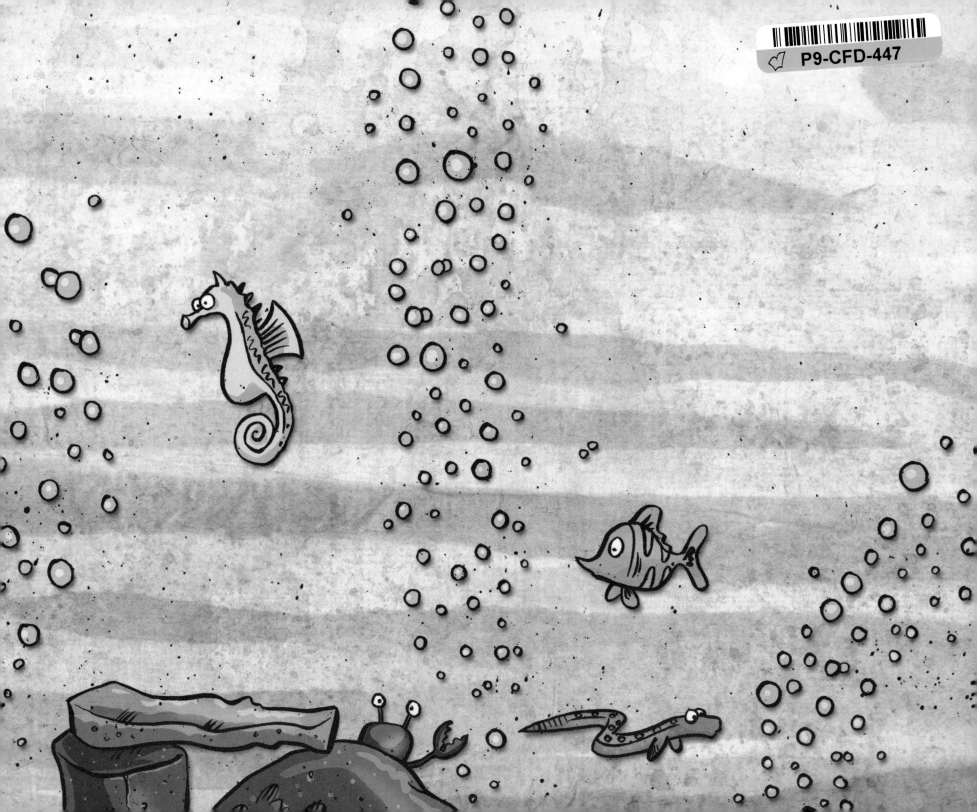

The Fish Who Could Fly

The Fish Who Could Fly
A Tale of Discovery

Written by

Leonard W. Lambert

Illustrated by Kevin Cook

 Arnica Creative Services
Portland, Oregon

Publisher's Cataloging-in-Publication Data

Lambert, Leonard W.
The Fish Who Could Fly: A Tale of Discovery. —1st ed.
p. cm.
j811.6
1. Marine animals–Juvenile poetry. 2. Children's poetry, American. 3. Rhyming stories
I. Kevin Cook, ill. II. Title

Library of Congress Control Number: 2014907299
ISBN: 978-0-9838168-5-0

Acknowledgments

I would like to thank the following people for their hard work and support:

Megan Lambert for being my partner every waking, sleeping and dreaming step of the way, you're truly the brains of the operation and the realist; Kevin Cook for bringing the Flying Fish to life in a way I never imagined; Ross Hawkins for believing in my work and his vision for educating youth (and for hugging everybody longer than normal); Gloria Martinez for her impeccable editing, organization and marketing advice; Aaron Hood-Foster for his unequalled visual skills and support; Aimee Genter-Gilmore for her design ability and gifted eye. Also to Dave Sizer for his artistic web and print design and just being a great friend; Lori Reed for introducing me to such a wonderful team at Arnica Creative Services and her attention to detail, without Lori this would not have happened! And to Frank Reed for being the best friend a guy could have. Neil Reilly, you have taught me more than you know and I appreciate all your wisdom and advice. To all my friends and family that have given so much support and contribution throughout this process, my mom, Gwen for giving me my creative brain, and my dad, Went, who gave me the gift of humor — I miss you every day and I could not have done it without you — thanks so much from the bottom of my heart, it is truly a dream come true. And lastly, Eva Lambert, thanks for being the best kid a parent could have. Keep asking those great questions so Dad can keep writing great books!

For Meg and Eva

You Can!

Ask yourself, "What is real?"
Is it only things you can feel?
A flying fish? A flying eel?
A laughing octopus, that can't be real?
Can a puppy smile? Can a kitten frown?
Can a giraffe stand on its head, upside down?
Can you do things you think you can't, and maybe say,
    instead, you can?
You can indeed, if you wish.
Just go and ask the flying fish.

Of all the things wet and all the things dry,
there once was a fish who thought he could fly.

Beneath the blue sea there lived a young fish,
that always looked up and said as he wished,

"I wonder what lies up above in the air?
I wish I could see but I know I don't dare."

Down below in the sea lived such beautiful things,
like a whale whose song carries far as he sings.

Fish of such color and splendor it's true.
But the little fish wondered,
"Do they live up there too?"

He asked the big octopus, "Can a fish really fly?"
The octopus laughed, "I've not seen one try."

The old grumpy grouper frowned as he said,
"Fish swim in water, get THAT in your head."

The little fish swam to his mom and he asked,
if a fish can do more than just swim, really fast?

His mom pulled him close and she looked in his eyes,
"A fish can do anything, you'd be surprised.
If you put your mind to it, and believe that it's true,
a fish can fly over the big ocean blue."

The other fish laughed and pointed their fins.
"How silly you are to think you can fly.
You are a fish, so don't even try."

It hurt to hear them laugh as they had,
the little fish turned and he
swam away sad.

"I'LL show you I can! I'LL show you you're wrong!
I have these fine fins and a tail that is strong!"

With a hold of his breath and a flick of his tail
he spread his fins wide and started to sail.

As he hovered above the ocean down there,
he flew even higher on a breeze of warm air.

Over the land of green trees and plains of gold brown. The little fish marveled at life on the ground.

Up, up and away and still higher yet, the little fish flew by soft clouds that were wet.

"Egad, look at that!" The sailor did scream,
as the fish flew 'round the bow, and the beam.

As he came down to rest in his watery home,
Mom's great big wide fins held him up as he shone.

The little fish taught all the others to fly,
and still to this day you can see them float by.

Out on the water with clear sunny days,
the fish love to fly in all different ways.

When valleys seem low and the mountains are high,
just remember the fish who thought he could fly.

Because all the things wet and all the things dry;
you'll never succeed if, at first, you don't try.

Flying fish lay their eggs on palm fronds that float out to sea. The palm frond becomes heavy with eggs. It sinks to the bottom where the baby flying fish are safe to hatch and grow.

Band wing flying fish

Pink wing flying fish

Tropical two wing flying fish

Flying fish use their tails to gather enough speed to glide above the water. Once the flying fish is going fast enough, it uses its large pectoral fins to break the water surface and rise into the air. They can glide the length of an entire football field; that is 300 feet! Flying fish use their special gliding ability to evade predators that want to eat them.

There are sixty-eight kinds of flying fish today and they live in oceans all over the world.

Octopuses have long arms called "tentacles." Each tentacle has over two hundred suckers that the octopus can control. An octopus uses its tentacles to search for food in small holes and cracks in coral reefs and rocky shores. It also uses its tentacles to swim through the water or to give someone a great big hug! Can you count how many tentacles the octopus has (hint: the number of tentacles is the first part of their name, "octo").

Octopuses are very shy, gentle creatures and they can change their shape and color to easily fit their surroundings. They can make themselves look like a rock, or become very bright and colorful to warn others to stay away. Can you see how the octopus below changed its colors?

Octopuses live in all parts of the ocean, but the largest octopus is the Giant Pacific Octopus. They live in the Pacific Northwest of the United States and near the country of Japan. A Giant Pacific Octopus can weigh up to 150 pounds and wrap its tentacles around a small car! How much do you weigh?

Was it okay for the grumpy grouper and the others to make fun of the flying fish?

You might think a grouper gets its name from swimming around in a group, but the word grouper means fish in Portuguese. Grouper live in warm, tropical water and coral reefs and there are many types. Although not always grumpy, grouper are tough fish and they can grow very large. The Goliath grouper is the largest, weighing up to 800 pounds.

The largest animal on the planet is the blue whale. It is almost 100 feet long and weighs over 125 tons. That is as long as two school buses and as heavy as twenty adult elephants! Blue whales are extremely rare, as only a few are left in the wild ocean, so if you ever see one, consider yourself lucky! Whales breathe through a hole at the top of their head called a "blowhole." A blue whale can hold its breath for 20 minutes at a time while swimming underwater. They communicate through song, which is the loudest noise in the animal kingdom and travels for miles underwater. They use their blowhole to create sounds that make up the whale's song.

Where do you live? Can you find?

The Flying Fish · The Big Octopus · The Grumpy Grouper · The Blue Whale

Arctic Ocean

Asia

North America

Europe

Asia

Pacific Ocean

Atlantic Ocean

Africa

Indian Ocean

South America

Indian Ocean

Australia

N

W   E

S

Southern Ocean

Antarctica

The Silver Swan

Michael Morpurgo

Illustrated by Christian Birmingham

PHYLLIS FOGELMAN
NEW YORK

For dear Carol
M.M.

To Ben
C.B.

Some information about swans and foxes

The Mute Swan is recognizable by a knob at the base of the beak. Originally brought over from Europe, domesticated swans can be found in parks all over North America. There is also a sizable population of swans that have become wild; they live primarily on the Atlantic coast of the United States. They are very aggressive in the breeding season, and are monogamous. A pair will stay together until death. They are loving in their courtship, and work together to build the nest, the cob (the male) often doing the gathering, the pen (the female) the arranging. The cob looks after the pen during incubation, and once the cygnets are hatched will help feed and protect them. Mute swans are rarely heard to make a sound.

The Common Red Fox generally lives in burrows. It lies low during the day, coming out to hunt at dusk or at night. The vixen (female) will produce a litter of between three and eight cubs that are dependent on her for survival for several months. The American Red Fox is similar to its European brother, but is slightly larger and has longer hair.

First published in the United States in 2000
by Phyllis Fogelman Books
An imprint of Penguin Putnam Books for Young Readers
345 Hudson Street
New York, New York 10014

Published in Great Britain
by Transworld Publishers

The text of this book is set in Bernhardt Modern.
Printed in Singapore
First Edition
1 3 5 7 9 10 8 6 4 2

Library of Congress information available upon request

The full-color artwork was prepared
using chalk pastels.

I live on my father's farm, far from anywhere and anyone. But it is not a lonely life, for I find my friends in the birds and animals that I see out in the woods and fields and lakes around the farm. These are all the friends I need. I love to be near them, to be among them, to feel as if I am one of them.

A swan came to my lake one day, a silver swan. I was fishing for trout in the moonlight. She came flying in above me, her wings singing in the air. She circled the lake twice, and then landed, silver, silver in the moonlight.

I stood and watched her as she arranged her wings behind her and sailed out over the lake, making it entirely her own. I stayed as late as I could, quite unable to leave her.

I went down to the lake every day after that, not to fish for trout, but simply to watch my silver swan.

In those early days I took great care not to frighten her away, keeping myself still and hidden in the shadow of the alders. But even so, she knew I was there—I was sure of it.

Within a week I would find her cruising along the lakeside, waiting for me when I arrived in the early mornings. I took to bringing some bread crusts with me. She would look sideways at them at first, rather disdainfully. Then, after a while, she reached out her neck, snatched them out of the water, and made off with them in triumph.

One day I dared to dunk the bread crusts for her, dared to try to feed her by hand. She took all I offered her and came back for more. She was coming close enough now for me to be able to touch her neck. I would talk to her as I stroked her. She really listened— I know she did.

I never saw the cob arrive. He was just there swimming beside her one morning out on the lake. You could see the love between them even then. The princess of the lake had found her prince. When they drank, they dipped their necks together, as one. When they flew, their wings beat together, as one.

She knew I was there, I think, still watching. But she did not come to see me again, nor to have her bread crusts. I tried to be more glad for her than sad for me, but it was hard.

As winter tried, and failed, to turn to spring, they began to make a home on the small island, way out in the middle of the lake. I could watch them now only through my binoculars. I was there every day I could be—no matter what the weather.

Things were happening. They were no longer busy just preening themselves, or feeding, or simply gliding out over the lake, taking their reflections with them. Between them they were building a nest—a clumsy, messy excuse for a nest, it seemed to me—set on a reedy knoll near the shore of their island.

It took them several days to construct. Neither ever seemed quite satisfied with the other's work. Either a twig was too big, or too small, or perhaps just not in the right place. There were no arguments as such, as far as I could see. But my silver swan would rearrange things, tactfully, when her cob wasn't there. And he would do the same when she wasn't there.

Then, one bright, cold morning with the ground beneath my feet hard with a late and unexpected frost, I arrived to see my silver swan enthroned at last on her nest, her cob proudly patrolling the lake close by.

I knew there were foxes about even then. I had heard their cries often enough echoing through the night. I had seen their footprints in the snow. But I had never seen one out and about, until now.

It was dusk. I was on my way back home from the lake, coming up through the woods, when I spotted a family of five cubs, their mother sitting on guard nearby. Unseen and unsmelled by them, I crouched down where I was and watched.

I could see at once that they were starving, some of them already too weak even to pester their mother for food. But I could see too that she had none to give—she was thin and rangy herself. I remember thinking then: That's one family of foxes that's not likely to make it, not if the spring doesn't come soon, not if this winter goes on much longer.

But the winter did go on that year, on and on.

I thought little more of the foxes. My mind was on other things, more important things. My silver swan and her cob shared the sitting duties and the guarding duties, never leaving the precious nest long enough for me even to catch sight of the eggs, let alone count them. But I could count the days, and I did.

As the day approached I made up my mind I would go down to the lake, no matter what, and stay there until it happened—however long that might take. But the great day dawned foggy. Out of my bedroom window, I could barely see across the farmyard.

I ran all the way down to the lake. From the lakeside I could see nothing of the island, nothing of the lake, only a few feet of limpid gray water lapping at the muddy shore. I could hear the muffled *aarking* of a heron out in the fog, and the distant piping of a moorhen. But I stayed to keep watch, all that day, all the next.

I was there in the morning two days later when the fog began at last to lift and the pale sun to come through. The island was there again. I turned my binoculars at once on the nest. It was deserted. They were gone. I scanned the lake, still mist-covered in places. Not a ripple. Nothing.

Then, out of nothing they appeared—my silver swan, her cob, and four cygnets, coming straight toward me. As they came toward the shore, they turned and sailed right past me. I swear she was showing them to me, parading them. They both swam with such easy power, the cygnets bobbing along in their wake. But I had counted wrong. There was another one, hitching a ride between his mother's folded wings. A snug little swan, I thought, littler than the others, perhaps. A lucky little swan.

That night the wind came in from the north and the lake froze over. It stayed frozen. I wondered how they would manage. But I need not have worried. They swam about, keeping a pool of water near the island clear of ice. They had enough to eat, enough to drink. They would be fine. And every day the cygnets were growing. It was clear now that one of them was indeed much smaller, much weaker. But he was keeping up. He was coping. All was well.

Then, silently, as I slept one night, it snowed outside. It snowed on the farm, on the trees, on the frozen lake. I took bread crusts with me the next morning, just in case, and hurried down to the lake. As I came out of the wood I saw the fox's paw-prints in the snow. They were leading down toward the lake.

I was running, stumbling through the drifts, dreading all along what I might find.

The fox was stalking around the nest. My silver swan was standing her ground over her young, neck lowered in attack, her wings beating the air frantically, furiously. I shouted. I screamed. But I was too late and too far away to help.

Quick as a flash the fox darted in, had her by the wing and was dragging her away. I ran out onto the ice. I felt it crack and give suddenly beneath me. I was knee-deep in the lake then, still screaming—but the fox would not be put off. I could see the blood—red, bright red on the snow. The five cygnets were scattering in their terror. My silver swan was still fighting. But she was losing, and there was nothing I could do.

I heard the sudden singing of wings above me. The cob! The cob flying in, diving to attack. The fox took one look upward, released her victim, and scampered off over the ice, chased all the way by the cob.

For some moments I thought my silver swan was dead. She lay so still on the snow. But then she was on her feet and limping back to her island, one wing flapping feebly, the other trailing, covered in blood and useless. She was gathering her cygnets about her. They were all there. She was enfolding them, loving them, when the cob came flying back to her, landing awkwardly on the ice.

He stood over her all that day and would not leave her side. He knew she was dying. So, by then, did I. I had nothing but revenge and murder in my heart. Time and again, as I sat there at the lakeside, I thought of taking my father's gun and going into the woods to hunt down the killer fox. But then I would think of her cubs and would know that she was only doing what a mother fox had to do.

For days I kept my cold, sad vigil by the lake. The cob was sheltering the cygnets now, my silver swan sleeping nearby, her head tucked under her wing. She scarcely ever moved.

I wasn't there, but I knew the precise moment she died. I knew it because she sang it. It's quite true what they say about swans singing only when they die. I was at home. I had been sent out to fetch logs for the fire before I went up to bed. The world about me was crisp and bright under the moon. The song was clearer and sweeter than any human voice, than any birdsong, I had ever heard before. So sang my silver swan and died.

I expected to see her lying dead on the island the next morning. But she was not there. The cob was sitting still as a statue on his nest, his five cygnets around him.

I went looking for her. I picked up the trail of feathers and blood at the lakeside, and followed where I knew it must lead, up through the wood. I approached silently. The fox cubs were frolicking fat and furry in the sunshine, their mother close by, intent on her grooming. There was a terrible wreath of white feathers nearby, and telltale feathers too on her snout. She was trying to shake them off. How I hated her.

I ran at her. I picked up stones. I hurled them. I screamed at her. The foxes vanished into the undergrowth and left me alone in the woods. I picked up a silver feather, and cried tears of such raw grief, such fierce anger.

Spring came at long last the next day, and melted the ice. The cob and his five cygnets were safe. After that I came less and less to the lake. It wasn't quite the same without my silver swan. I went there only now and again, just to see how he was doing, how they were all doing.

At first, to my great relief, it seemed as if he was managing well enough on his own. Then one day I noticed there were only four cygnets swimming alongside him, the four bigger ones. I don't know what happened to the smaller one. He just wasn't there. Not so lucky, after all.

The cob would sometimes bring his cygnets to the lakeside to see me. I would feed them when he came, but then after a while he just stopped coming.

The weeks passed and the months passed, and the cygnets grew and flew. The cob scarcely left his island now. He stayed on the very spot I had last seen my silver swan. He did not swim, he did not feed, he did not preen himself. Day by day it became clearer that he was pining for her, dying for her.

Now my vigil at the lakeside was almost constant again. I had to be with him, to see him through. It was what my silver swan would have wanted, I thought.

So I was there when it happened. A swan flew in from nowhere one day, down onto the glassy stillness of the lake. She landed right in front of him. He walked down into the lake, settled into the water and swam out to meet her. I watched them look each other over for just a few minutes. When they drank, they dipped their necks together, as one. When they flew, their wings beat together, as one.

Five years later and they're still
together. Five years later and I still
have the feather from my silver swan.
I take it with me wherever I go.
I always will.